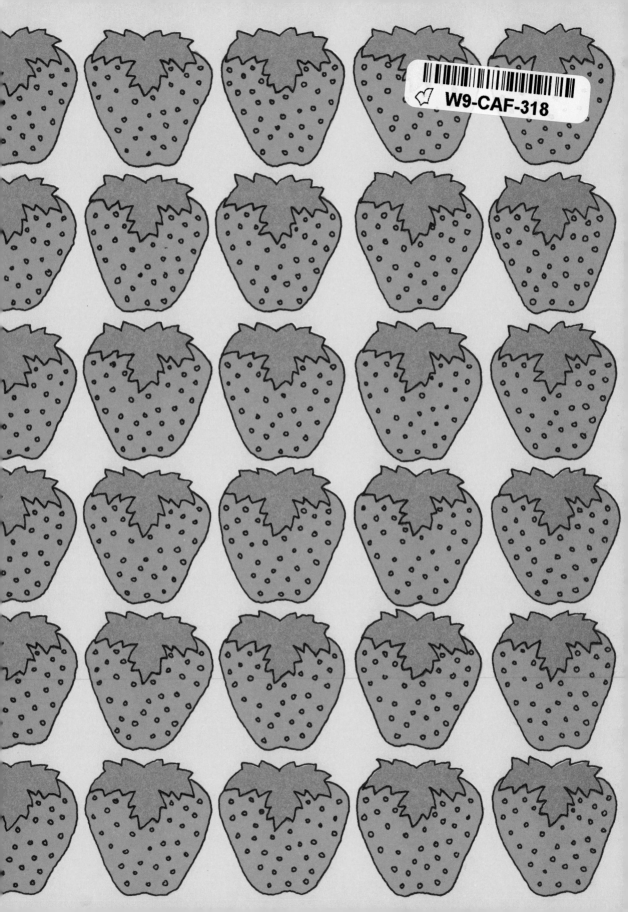

this
strawberry book
belongs to

Megan
Cook

*this book
is for
Christopher
and the
Walrus in
his closet*

Library of Congress Catalog Card Number: 74-81377
ISBN: Trade 0-88470-012-7, Library 0-88470-013-5

Weekly Reader Books' Edition

a noise in the closet

by Richard Hefter

a strawberry book ®

One night, after he had been tucked in bed,
Christopher heard a noise coming from the closet
in the corner of his room.

Christopher slid quietly out of bed and tiptoed to
the closet. He opened the door very slowly
and looked inside.

There was a very large walrus standing there.
"What are you doing in my closet?" asked Christopher.
The walrus tipped his hat.
"I am the Ringmaster of the Famous Traveling
Closet Circus. We perform only in children's closets!"

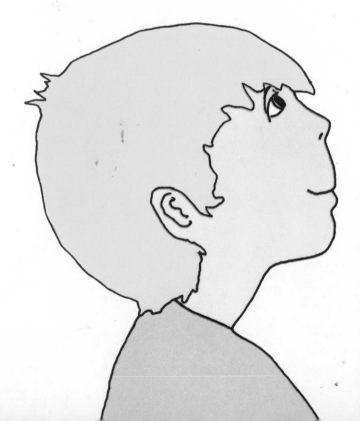

Then the walrus blew a loud tweet on his whistle
and shouted, "Follow me!"
He stepped behind the pants and coats.
Christopher followed him.
Behind the clothes were a chair and a large circus ring.

In the center of the ring was the walrus, who shouted, "The Famous Traveling Closet Circus is proud to present the stupendous Madame Chicken and her well trained pony."

A white pony pranced into the ring. As it trotted around and around, a chicken did all sorts of tricks on the pony's back. She did somersaults and flips. She stood on her head. She jumped through a hoop.

When she was finished, there were dancing bears
and juggling alligators, high wire kangaroos
and acrobat elephants.
Christopher clapped and cheered.

There were hippopotamus clowns and trapeze turtles.
Christopher clapped and cheered.

Then the walrus stepped into the ring. He blew his whistle. "The Famous Traveling Closet Circus presents the most fantastic lion tamer anywhere. The Amazing Magnifico, the bravest puppy in the world!"

Just then, the chicken ran into the ring and shouted,
"I have very bad news about the lion tamer!"
She jumped onto the walrus' shoulder and whispered
something in his ear.

"This is terrible news," moaned the walrus. "The circus is ruined!" And a big wet tear rolled out of his eye. "What's wrong," asked Christopher, " why are you crying?"

"The Amazing Magnifico," the walrus cried, "won't go into the cage with the lion. He says he doesn't feel well. Without a lion tamer the circus is ruined. I wish we could find someone brave enough to go into the cage with the lion!"

Christopher looked around and saw everyone with sad faces.
Then he looked into the cage straight at the lion.
The lion smiled at Christopher.
"I," said Christopher, "will be the lion tamer."

Christopher took a chair and a hat and marched right into the lion's cage.

The lion jumped up on a stand. Christopher held up his hand.
The lion stood on his hind legs. Then Christopher had
the lion walk on a narrow pole. The lion shook hands with
Christopher and grinned.

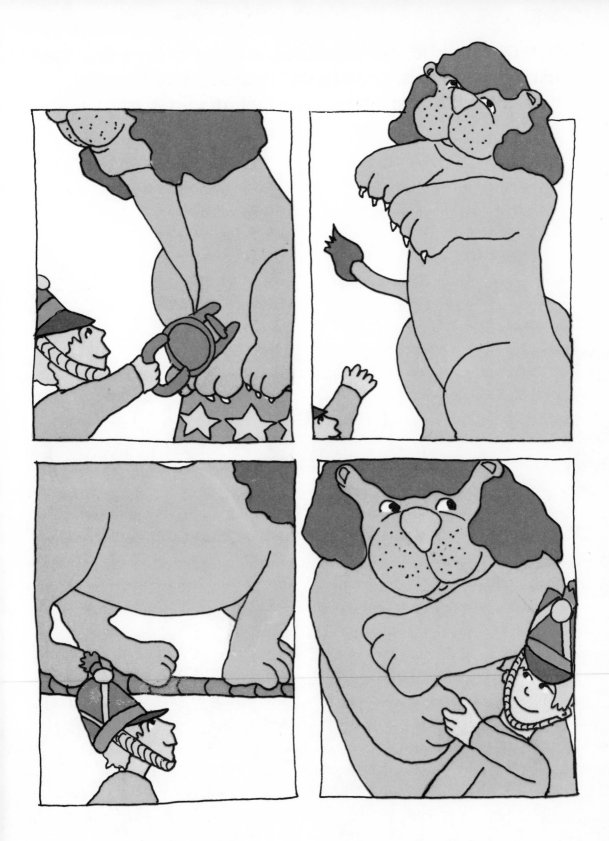

When Christopher came out of the cage, everyone clapped and cheered. The walrus gave him a big medal on a shiny ribbon. And on the medal it said:

THE BRAVEST
LION TAMER
IN THE CLOSET

Christopher sat down in his chair.
The walrus stepped into the ring and said,
"The show is over. We'll be back again next year.
We hope you had a good time."

Then the walrus took Christopher out of the closet and back to his bed. He tucked Christopher in, and waved goodnight.

In the morning, Christopher jumped out of bed and ran
to the closet. He opened the door and looked inside.
Everything looked the same, there was no sign of the circus.

Then Christopher looked down.
Around his neck, on a shiny ribbon, was a bright
yellow medal. It said:

THE BRAVEST
LION TAMER
IN THE CLOSET

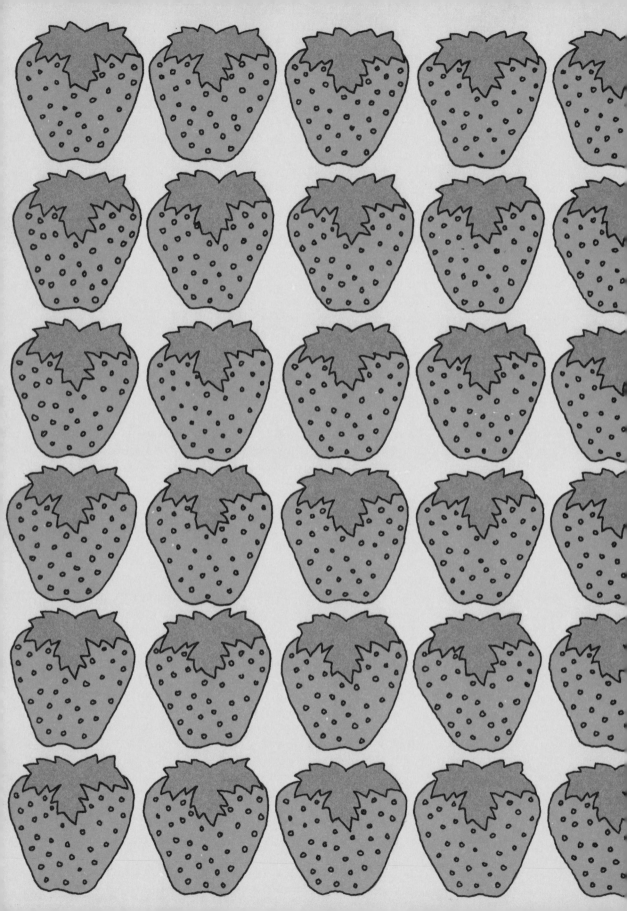